I0539080

~~~~~

O.G. It's Christmas!

An Ocean Grove (short) Mystery

Heath P. Boice

~~~~~

Seabreeze Press

Rochester, NY

O.G. It's Christmas! An Ocean Grove (short) Mystery

ISBN-13: 978-0615815053
ISBN-10: 0615815057

This is a work of fiction. Unless otherwise noted, the example companies, organizations, products, people, and events depicted herein are fictitious and no association with any real company, organization, product, person, or event is intended or should be inferred.

Printed in the United States of America.

For information about film, reprint, or other subsidiary rights, please contact: permissions@seabreezepress.com

Seabreeze Press in an independent publishing house.

Seabreeze Press
Rochester, NY
www.seabreezepress.com
contact@seabreezepress.com

Library of Congress Cataloging-in-Publication data available.

Also by

Heath P. Boice

~~~~~

Missing by the Midway

Ocean Grove Mysteries Book 1

Buried by the Boardwalk

Ocean Grove Mysteries Book 2

Dedication

To Ocean Grove and holiday magic.

Acknowledgements

I would like to thank my readers for welcoming Dean Doug and the Asbury College gang into your worlds. This book was largely motivated by people asking for more Ocean Grove Mysteries. I hope this fits the bill for a little while!

~1~

Christmas down the shore does not look like a

traditional snow-covered Christmas card. The
temperatures are often still in the upper forties with nary
a snowflake in sight. People still run their dogs on the
beach, and bikes don't get hidden away for the season
until the first snowfall, which sometimes forgets to arrive.
But I remember one Christmas in particular that was

different. The first snow fell just after Thanksgiving, and a cold snap gripped Ocean Grove for the entire holiday season.

It's fabled that holiday magic exists. And that year, I experienced it first hand for the first and only time in my life. It wasn't magic out of a hat, but out of the heart. Whose heart? I'm not sure. I suppose that adds to the magic.

As the Dean of Students at Asbury College in Ocean Grove, New Jersey, and a town resident, I love my walk to work. I often see friends and neighbors along my route, and even get to run an errand or two before I reach campus. I remember the day that everything happened was the Wednesday before Christmas. I remember, because it was a day never to be forgotten.

I shuffled through the snow-covered sidewalks, on December 23, ready to close out another semester and send the students from Asbury College home for Christmas break. A major snowstorm was in the forecast, and before I went to campus, I made a quick stop at the Ocean Grove Post Office on Main Avenue to mail

Christmas gifts to my mom in Bennington, Vermont. I
knew that they wouldn't arrive in time for Christmas, but
given the craziness of the academic year, I had done the
best that I could. As I wrestled with the Post Office door,
trying not to destroy the gifts before they arrived, I saw
an elderly woman approaching. She was barely moving,
her gait slow and methodical, but she was wearing a
bright red cloak, which caught my eye.

I waited, holding the door for her, clutching my
packages for dear life while she made her way to the door
dragging a rolling shopping cart behind her. As she
began her entrance, I fumbled one of my packages,
almost knocking her over; so much for my good
samaritanship. "I'm so sorry," I uttered, trying to
compose myself and gather my belongings.

"No need to be sorry, Dean Doug, I appreciate
you holding the door for me. Like you, I'm trying to get
these packages mailed before the storm hits."

I tried to get a good look at her face, which was
mostly covered by her cloak. All I could see was an aged
chin, and some snow white ringlets falling from her hood.

"Ma'am," I said, pushing the door wider with my butt, "do I know you?" As the Dean of Students at Ocean Grove's only College, I am used to the campus and town communities calling me "Dean Doug." My full name is Douglas Carter-Connors. My wife, Barbara and I hyphenated our last names (I was the Carter) when we married. Our son, Ethan, also shares the Carter-Connors moniker.

"Well," the lady said, exposing a blue eye and warm expression from under her hood, "I don't think we've ever officially met, but I surely know you. You're practically a legend around here." I laughed, out of discomfort, much more loudly than usual.

"I doubt that," I said, "but I appreciate the thought."

"Don't be so humble, my dear," the admiring stranger responded. Surely blushing, and thankful that the brisk ocean breeze that whipped my face masked my embarrassment, I simply smiled, "You have a wonderful day."

She nodded, wheeled herself inside, and headed toward the open clerk. I followed, for some odd reason, hoping to remove myself from my crimson stranger's presence. She weirded me out, just a little bit. But in Ocean Grove, even a few days before Christmas, there was only one clerk open at 9am. My new friend conducted her business, mailing a few letters, some packages, and buying some stamps, and then left the window vacating a space for me. As she walked past me, she nudged me with her arm and said, "Thank you again, Dean Doug. You have a busy day ahead of you."

The statement struck me as odd, since most of my students were heading out of town and by the end of the day, campus would be a virtual ghost town. I looked at her in a nonchalantly and said, "Thank you, but actually, most of our students will be gone by tonight. I'm looking forward to some quiet."

My new friend eyed me thoughtfully, then winked and said, "Dean Doug, you possess a gift unlike most. Although sometimes eager to please, and wary of things new, your conscience always leads the way, especially on our coast." She then moved faster than I had seen her previously, and exited the Post Office, wheeling her black cart behind her.

I didn't think much of it then, but by the end of the day realized that she was right. I was in for a busy day. Twenty-four hours filled with worry, excitement, and holiday magic. It is a chapter in my life that I call, "O.G., it's Christmas!"

~2~

I mailed my packages, said a prayer that my

mother would receive her Christmas gifts unharmed to ease the pain that we weren't visiting, and headed to campus. As I trudged through the snow, my strange new friend's comments plagued me, even though I couldn't remember them verbatim. Something like, 'eager to please, worried about new things along the coast.' What was she talking about?

As I walked toward my office on the second floor of the Student Center on the Asbury College campus, I received an inkling that my red-coated friend was right. The day was not going to be a quiet one. I could see my trusty assistant, Judy, through the plate glass windows of the Dean of Students Office (DOSO) suite motioning to me from her desk. She looked like an air traffic controller with a jet black bouffant and a very loud

Christmas sweater. I hurried my pace and opened the door to the suite. "Turn right around, mister," Judy exhaled, "your presence is needed in the chapel."

"The chapel? Why?"

"I'm not sure, but some students are there and something happened. They need you right away."

"Did they call security?"

"If they didn't, I will. Now go!" Judy gestured in broad sweeping motions, reminding me of the Wicked Witch of the West ushering the flying monkeys away, in an ugly Christmas sweater, no less.

I walked as quickly as I could to Asbury's chapel, which was halfway across campus. Although Asbury College was founded in the Methodist tradition, we are private and do not hold a particular religious slant. Our chapel is located in the basement of Wilson Hall, our main administration building. It is a dark space that smells of old wood and looks like something out of a medieval castle, and in fact, it was imported from a castle in Europe. I ran into Wilson Hall, stomped the snow off my boots, and shuffled quickly downstairs to find the students who had called.

"Dean Doug," I heard as I hit the bottom of the stairs, "hurry!" I looked to see two students in the hallway adjacent to the chapel. "What's wrong?" I asked. Neither student responded, but one grabbed me by the hand and led me inside the sanctuary.

As I entered, even in the panicked nature of my visit, I was struck by the Chapel's beauty. An oversized nativity set had been on the alter nestled on a bed of pine boughs. A group of six students were standing in front of the scene, staring at it. Although I was filled with a sense of urgency upon making my entrance, the mood of the room was calm. No one spoke, as all eyes were affixed on the crèche. I looked around quizzically, "What's the matter?" Still no one moved.

Finally, an African-American student whom I did not know pointed to the manger. I walked closer, still struck by the beautiful sight. Everything seemed to be in place. Two sheep, a cow, a donkey, a poor stable boy, Mary and Joseph, all focusing on baby Jesus who was semi-covered in his swaddling clothes. What was I missing? As I continued my mental game of, "What's wrong with this picture," one student fell to her knees in front of the cradle. It was then that I saw it.

The baby Jesus moved.

*****

Seeing the staccato movement of the baby's hand also caused me to fall to my knees—not out of reverence, but shock. I also wanted to get a closer look. Once on my knees, I shuffled up to the cradle. The baby was wrapped in a traditional hospital newborn blanket-- white with muted red and blue stripes with wisps of brown hair framing the face. Although not an expert, he appeared to be a newborn. I turned around to look at my mesmerized companions.

"Where did he come from?" I asked in a hushed voice, not expecting an answer. One of the young men behind me shrugged, and pointed toward the sky. I was as religious as the next guy (well, maybe not), but I had no illusion that the baby who lay before me was shipped from Heaven. I rose from my semi-recumbent position, careful not to disturb the sleeping baby, and turned to the group, "How long ago did you find him?"

"About fifteen minutes ago," Jenny Robins, one of my Resident Assistants responded. "We came in this morning to clean-up the chapel after last night's service and before we leave for break. He was... he was just here."

"So you opened-up the chapel this morning and he was here?"

"The chapel was already open, Dean Doug," Jessica Philmore chimed in. "We were going to call security to unlock it, but when we got here, the doors were already unlocked." A couple of the students looked nervously at each other. At that moment, the relative calm of the chapel was broken by loud footsteps and the jingling of keys. We all turned in unison and saw the director of Campus Security, Tina "Quacky" Braggish, ambling her squat frame into the chapel. The hem of her uniform's overcoat hovered over the floor by a mere inch, making her appear like a royal blue Angel tree topper. On the top of her head rested her officer's hat, covered in plastic and dripping with new snow. Clearly, the impending Nor'easter had begun.

"I got a call that there was an emergency!" Quacky shouted as if she were at a carnival, and not a chapel. Her outburst startled the baby who immediately started to cry. Although the look on Quacky's face was priceless, I resisted the urge to laugh and instinctively reached down and picked up the baby. Although my son, Ethan, was six, I had not lost my 'daddy jiggle' expertise as I simultaneously rocked and bounced the newborn to pacify him. Quacky stopped cold at the sight, jaw agape, still dripping, "Doug, what is *that*?"

"It's a baby, Tina," I replied, still jiggling.

"I know it's a baby," Tina called, starting to move closer. "Why do you have it?"

"The students found him lying in the manger this morning." As I spoke, the newborn started to squirm—I suspected that feeding time was imminent. "We should probably call an ambulance and get him to Jersey Shore Medical Center, don't you think?" My idea seemed to knock Quacky out of her daze. "Doug, in the last thirty minutes, six inches of snow has fallen. We're supposed to get a foot an hour-- the roads are gridlocked. Does he appear to be injured?"

"I haven't really looked—but I'm sure he's going to want to eat very soon. We're going to have to find him some formula." At that, one of the young women spoke hesitantly, "I know where there's some formula... I think." One of her peers quickly turned her head and stared at her wide-eyed. "Uh, no," she responded to her friend, "I volunteer for the Women's Center on-campus. We've been collecting things for new mothers at the women's shelter in Asbury Park. It's all being stored at the Student Health Center." Although I wasn't sure what sort of non-verbal communication was going on between the students, I was happy to hear that we had found a solution for our baby.

"That's great," I said. "Chief Braggish, can you go to the Health Center, grab some of the formula and a bottle?"

"Sure thing, Doug," Quacky said already making her way out the door. "But it might take me a little bit with all of the snow. Come with me, miss," Quacky spoke to the young woman. I'll need your help in locating the necessary items." The student nodded, and Quacky huffed importantly, "We'll be back as soon as we can."

Just as Tina and the student exited, the lights in the chapel started to flicker, antique wall sconces coughing out light, then forced into darkness briefly before regaining life. Even from the basement of Wilson Hall, I could hear the wind raging outside, carrying with it what I imagined to be heavy white shrouds of snow. "Everybody freeze!" came Tina's voice from the hallway followed by her head popping back inside the doorway. "Okay, folks," she said, holding her hands out in sweeping stopping motions. "I'm going to clear the chapel. If we lose power, I don't want anyone down here in the basement. You'd break your necks in the dark trying to find your way out."

"Thanks, Tina," I said, continuing my rocking motions while our little Asbury savior continued his slumber. "I think we should take this little guy over to my office. C'mon everyone, let's go."

"Good call, Doug," Tina said putting on her gloves. "The storm's really firing up. Why don't I give you and the little guy a ride to your office before we head over to the Health Center. Kids, you bundle up and meet the Dean at his office."

As I wrapped my coat over the baby swaddling him in preparation for fighting the elements, I also noticed that something was going on between the students. The group was huddled together speaking in hushed tones—something was up, but I couldn't focus on them at that moment. I had another priority sitting in my arms and I wanted to get him settled before he woke up, or before the storm got so bad that I couldn't relocate him from the chapel.

~3~

I barely walked into the Dean of Students Office

suite before Judy scooped the baby out of my arms. A mother of five, Judy knew her way around an infant and I was happy to have her expertise and take the lead. "You don't seem surprised that I come bearing gifts," I said, taking-off my coat.

"I have my sources," Judy said, cooing at the bundle. "Received a call just before the phones went out. Oh, by the way, the phones went out. Has the baby been quiet all this time?"

"Yes," I said proudly, "hasn't made a peep."

"Hmmmmm…" Judy said, leaning in closer to the baby's face. "That's trouble. With all this commotion, and the cold, I can't believe he's still sleeping."

"Maybe he's been through a lot," I offered hopefully. "We did just find him in a wooden manger in the middle of a blizzard."

"Well, he's no newborn, I can tell you that. At least, he wasn't just born. He's at least four weeks old. And by the smell of him, he needs a diaper change. That's a good sign. What are we going to do for diapers?"

"Quacky went to Health Services to get some formula and hopefully diapers. The students have been collecting things for the local women's shelter. She's bringing things back." As if the prospect of a clean diaper and some breakfast was appealing, the baby started to stir, then cry for the first time in our possession.

"They-uh, they-uh," Judy jiggled, pulling out her infamous Brooklyn accent. "Well, that's a relief, glad he's crying. It's a good sign. But that formula better be here soon."

"Shouldn't be too long," I said hopefully.

"I wouldn't count on that," came Jessica Philmore's voice from behind me. The students filed into DOSO, dripping wet with snow. "There must be almost a foot out there already. I'm not sure Chief Braggish's security mobile is gonna make it through."

"Yeah," said one of the guys, "as soon as Facilities' plows, the sidewalks are covered-over again. They can't keep up!"

I looked out of our suite and saw the nearly white-out conditions, "I've never seen anything like this down the shore. It came on so fast!" As if in agreement, the baby started to wail and Judy jumped into action, "Kids, do you have any of those left over Student Government tee shirts in the SG office?"

"Sure," said Tommy Johnson.

"Good," Judy responded. "Go grab a few. We need to change this baby."

"You're going to use our tee shirts?" Tommy asked, incredulous.

"Do you have a better solution? If you'd rather me use your Abercrombie tee, take it off, fella." Judy looked over her half specs showing just how much experience she had in handling children, from infants to teens.

"I'll be right back," Tommy ran out the door. Judy continued to rock the baby by instinct, not duty. Never being the greatest at timing, I looked at the group, "So, where do we think this baby came from?" The students looked at each other nervously, but Judy quickly mused, "Dean Doug, you have a son, haven't you figured that out yet?" Judy always knew how to make me blush.

"Judy, I was asking beyond the cliché," was all I could muster. "Who is the mother of this baby? Does anyone know?"

"He was just *there*," Jessica jumped in. "We just *found* him." As she said this, it struck me as odd, since Asbury was closing for break, why were students in the chapel? I decided to ease into that one. "So, can you tell me how you found the baby?" Again, more looks between the students, then Jessica jumped back in, "We went to the chapel this morning, you know early before we all left for break, to celebrate Christmas together."

"But someone said that you went to clean up from last night's Lessons and Carols service," I pushed. "Wasn't that celebration enough?"

"Oh yeah, well it was both," Charley, another student chimed in," we were looking for something more personal. Just between us…and then the cleaning, of course."

"And you all decided to gather in the chapel this morning, before a blizzard, to celebrate and clean?"

"Exactly!" Jessica offered, a bit too enthusiastically. Her peers noticed too, and shot her dagger glances. The story was just too ridiculous, and I had to call the question. "I appreciate your story," I said looking at faces who were not meeting my eye, "but I don't buy it." No one looked at me, but all of the students began fidgeting. "And I've got to remind you that we're in the middle of a crisis." A few eyes looked up at me, and I took that as a cue to continue, "It appears that a blizzard has started all around us. We have an infant to care for, without any food. And I would suspect that if he hasn't already, the Governor will call a state of emergency which means that all of us are stuck here. That said, I suspect that you know more than you are offering and I am asking, no, *pleading* that you tell me what is going on."

Jenny looked at Jessica and a few nods ensued. Jenny looked at me, "Okay, Dean Doug. It's kind of complicated, but we'll tell you what we know." I always marvel at how human beings know how to react to major life events. Instinctively, we sat down on the couches in the Dean of Students outer office to settle into the truth. I just hoped that it wasn't already too late.

~4~

"Tommy actually found her a few weeks ago," Jessica began.

"The baby?" I asked.

"No, Stephanie, the baby's mother. Tommy was volunteering at the teen center in Asbury Park and she was there. Stephanie told Tommy that she was homeless and had been staying with friends, but her friends had left town. She didn't have anywhere to go."

"So let me guess," I jumped in, "you brought her to campus." Jessica nodded, "Yes. We knew it was wrong, but when Tommy brought her to campus we also knew that we couldn't put her out on the street. As a Methodist college, it wouldn't be very Christian of us." Touché. They were playing the Christian card. As a private college in the Methodist tradition, I often marveled that we could be conveniently Christian, or conveniently private, at any given moment. Jessica continued, "Dean Doug, are you a Christian?" I ignored the question, thankfully relieved by Jenny. "But we didn't bring her to the residence halls," Jenny added, sounding like the quintessential Resident Assistant.

"So where did you bring her?"

"To the chapel," Jenny continued. "No one ever goes down there, and it's hidden away in the bottom of Wilson Hall." And within seconds, we went from conveniently Christian, to being conveniently private with a chapel that is hardly used. I couldn't argue, she was right. "The chapel was perfect," Jenny added, "Stephanie could come and go, and as long as she was back by the time Wilson Hall was locked for the night, she was fine."

"How long has she been living in the chapel?" I asked. Jenny looked uneasily at the group, "since just after Thanksgiving. Only a couple of weeks."

"A couple of weeks!" I blurted. "You don't know who this woman is. She was pregnant, and you allowed her to stay on Asbury's campus for 'a couple of weeks?'"

"We didn't know what else to do!" Jessica implored. If we said anything we knew that you would call the police and they would make Stephanie leave-- she might even go to jail!" I couldn't argue with her logic. "Alright," I said. "So let me guess, today you went down to get her settled before you left for break and…"

"She was gone!" Jessica cried. "She was gone, and her baby was left in the manger!"

"So where do you think Stephanie went?"

"We don't know," Charley joined the conversation. "All of her things are gone, with the exception of her baby, of course."

"And when did she have the baby?" I asked.

"She hadn't had the baby-- today was the first we saw him!" Jessica wailed. "What could have happened to Stephanie? Where did she go?" There were often pivotal

moments in conversations with students when they
stopped being the independent future leaders to post-
adolescents who needed the guidance of an adult. I
always found this an endearing quality. I didn't want to
share what I really thought. "Well," I started, "first we
need to get this baby changed and fed. I'm going to call
the Ocean Grove Police Department for more advice.
But before I do, is there anything else I need to know?"

The students shared a few more uncomfortable
stares between them. "Maybe," Charley reluctantly
offered. "Stephanie said that her parents were trying to
get custody of the baby. They thought she was unfit. So
if she's not around, where will the baby go?" What I
really wanted to know was that if Stephanie's parents
were so anxious to get her baby, why weren't they just as
determined to find and protect Stephanie? Before I could
respond, the baby began to wail again despite Judy's
expert jiggling. "Where is Quacky?" Judy called from
the copy room. "This baby is hungry!"

Right on time, Quacky ambled into the office,
soaking wet with two inches of snow on her plastic-

covered hat. "I got here as soon as I could, folks!" she said, out of breath. "It's terrible out there. Must be coming down at least two inches per hour. Here's the formula, Judy! I found a couple of bottles, too!" Judy emerged, still holding the baby, and approached Quacky. "He-yuh," she said, passing the baby off to me. "I need to get this formula going. You hold the prince while I do."

As Judy sashayed off toward the women's room around the corner, I held the baby noticing that he had once again become too silent for my liking. I jiggled him a little, and he stirred. But then, he began screaming. Quacky had leaned in to get a peek and dumped two inches of snow in his face. I was so relieved to hear his cries of anger that I didn't even mind. "I'm sorry Dean Doug," Quacky apologized, "I just wanted to see him! I'm sorry."

"No worries, Tina," I said, consoling the baby as I got the snow off of his face. "He's been through so much, a little snow won't hurt him. How does it look out there?"

"It's a nightmare," Quacky offered taking off her overcoat. "A total white-out. The roads are closed, the Governor's called a State of Emergency. I'm afraid all of us are stuck here for the foreseeable future."

"You mean we'll be here for Christmas?" Jessica asked.

"Maybe, honey," Quacky replied. "It's not safe for anyone to come get you, or for you to leave. It looks like we'll be celebrating Christmas together." As I heard the disappointment in the student's voices and held the baby, I silently answered Jessica's earlier question. Yes, I am a Christian, even though my doubts sometime overshadow my faith. Maybe, if we could save this baby and find his mother, just maybe my faith would be renewed.

~5~

Tommy returned with a few Student Government tee shirts as well as a handful of candy bars. "Mrs. Judy! Here are the tee shirts! I also grabbed some candy bars from the SG office in case we run out of food!"

"Judy's in the restroom," I said, jiggling the baby, "and I don't think he can have candy bars, yet."

"They're not for him, but for us! While I was upstairs I saw that New Jersey is in a state of emergency and we might need rations to survive." I chuckled at Tommy's thoughtfulness, but knew that we would not starve. The Student Center kitchen was one floor below us. "Thanks, Tommy," I said. "Good work." Just then Judy returned, bottle in hand, "You're off duty, Dean. Let me have the little fella." I handed him over to Judy who promptly sat down in one of the easy chairs and used her parenting expertise with the bottle. I was surprised that within seconds, the baby was gulping from the bottle.

"Wow," I marveled, "you're good." Judy looked at me over her spectacles, "and you evuh doubted me?"

"Never you, just biology. Glad he's eating." I turned to Quacky, "have you been in touch with the Ocean Grove PD?"

"Not yet," she sniffed, holding a steaming cup of hot chocolate, "I've been too busy."

"No worries, Tina," I responded, "mind if I call chief Morreale?"

"Not at all," Tina replied, still wiping snow and water from her face. I walked back to my office and dumped myself into my desk chair. I had only been at work for a few hours, and I was already exhausted. I remembered the words of the stranger in the Post Office, and wondered what "gift" I possessed. At the moment, I felt pretty insignificant. I picked up my desk phone, and dialed the Ocean Grove Police Department by memory.

It had been a busy year and I had needed their help more than I would have liked. On the second ring, the dispatcher picked up, "Ocean Grove Police Department, is this an emergency?"

I was taken aback by the question, "Well, uh,"

"Sir, we're in a state of emergency. Do you have one?"

"Uh, yes," I replied, "I do. But I'd like to speak with Police Chief Morreale, if I may."

"Who's calling, please?" the dispatcher came back, not lessening his intensity.

"Doug Carter-Connors from Asbury College," I said.

"Dean, is everyone safe at the moment? We're getting killed with calls."

"We're all fine, except that we found an abandoned infant on-campus. We're doing what we can to keep him alive." I thought that might grab his attention.

"Hold on, Dean," came the dispatcher's rattled voice. "Let me get the Chief." After a few moments and a couple of clicks, I was in the presence of the Chief's soothing vocals. "So, Dean Doug, another life or death emergency, I hear?

"You know me so well, chief. I hate to disappoint."

"Well as long as you're not dangling off a Ferris Wheel, things are looking up," the Chief was referring to one of my adventures a couple years prior. He continued, "So I hear that you've had a baby?"

"Well not me, but apparently some of my students took in a wayward mother who had one… and left him. We found him this morning lying in our chapel's manger."

"Appropriate for this time of year," the Chief responded and I could picture him lighting his pipe. "Is the baby healthy?"

"Well, he seems to be. Judy's feeding him now, and we've found enough formula to last us awhile."

"Where is the mom?"

"We don't know. The students say that she was bunking in our chapel for the past few weeks, but now she and all of her belongings, except for the baby, are gone."

"So where was the baby born?"

"Well, Judy estimates that he is about four weeks old, and she's my resident expert, but the kids say that as of a few days ago, they didn't think the baby had been born."

"That's a bit of a mystery," the chief mused.

"Well, you are talking about Asbury College. We seem to breed mystery."

"I can't argue. Do you know the mother's name?"

"All I know is *Stephanie*. I don't have a last name. I'll let you know if I learn more. Should we be doing anything else?"

"Well Doug, if the baby's safe and healthy, I would say keep him there. This storm has jammed all of our roads, and I bet it would take at least an hour to get an ambulance to you, and then another hour to go to Jersey Shore Medical."

"But Jersey Shore is only about eight miles away."

"That's right, which tells you how bad the roads are. Mother Nature was especially harsh by spraying all of our surfaces with a half inch of ice before dumping snow on top. I've never seen the roads like this before, Doug. If you can keep everyone safe on-campus, I advise that you do."

"We will try, Chief. Obviously if there is an emergency, we'll call for an ambulance. In the meantime, if you need to use any of our facilities as shelter, we are here and ready."

"I may just need to take you up on that offer. I can't imagine that the power's going to hold much longer and some of our seniors are going to be frantic."

"Then we'll begin to set up our Student Center for visitors. I'm not sure how comfortable it will be, but it will be dry, warm, and we'll have some food. I may be cooking, but we'll have food."

"Thanks a million," the Chief replied, "I'll be in touch." I hung up the phone and leaned back in my chair. This was surely a challenging situation, but we would persevere. Then I heard a scream from the outer office, and I wondered if I needed to rethink my position.

I ran from my desk and found the outer office in chaos. Judy was bobbing the swaddled baby, and the students were hovering over something on the floor. Quacky was observing, dripping hot chocolate from her chin. As I approached, I could see a young woman, probably about 20 years of age, lying on the floor. The students were surrounding her and doing what they could to make her comfortable. "Here's something for under your head," Jessica called. "And here is some water, drink it slowly," said Jenny. As I got closer, I could see why the fuss—the woman on the floor was pregnant. In fact, the woman on the floor was likely in labor.

"Do you know her?" Judy asked, swaddling a fulfilled and sleeping baby.

"Yes," Jessica answered. "This is Stephanie."

~6~

I looked at Judy, whom I knew shared my

wonder, 'if Stephanie was on the office floor having a

baby, whose baby was Judy holding?'

"Awwwwwww!" Stephanie screamed as the

students scurried to make her comfortable. Jessica asked,

"Stephanie, how can we help you?"

"Get this baby *out* of me!" Stephanie screamed.

She was pale and her blond hair was wet with melted

snow. Her blue sweatpants and unzipped puffy winter

snow jacket were also soaked and seemingly heavy on

her small frame. "I'm going to die!" Stephanie yelled,

and the students looked beseechingly at Judy and me for

some guidance. I looked toward Judy, "I'll take him, if

you take her," I said, and she took control immediately.

"Okay, kids, bring her to conference room A. Use your coats and whatever we have to make her comfortable on one of the conference room tables."

"Should we boil water and get clean sheets?" Charley yelled among the pandemonium. "Do you know what to do with boiled water and clean sheets?" Judy asked like a seasoned duty nurse. "No," Charley responded. "Then just get her in they-uh!" Judy called, being assertive, but not rude. That took talent.

"What are you going to do?" I called to Judy as she ran to the back copy room.

"I'm going to deliver that baby, unless you have another idea?"

"Judy, really?" I asked, panic rising in my voice. "Quacky, do you know how?" I didn't normally refer to Chief Tina Braggish by her commonly used nickname, but my sensitivity has lapsed. Luckily, Tina didn't seem to notice, "No," she replied, still clutching her cocoa, "but I can save someone from a burning building or a pool!"

"Thanks," I said, "if we run into anyone swimming, you'll be the first person we call. Judy, this is all you. Do you know how to deliver a baby?"

"No, but I've had five of my own and I watched a lot of General Hospital. Can you call Mary to see if she is on-campus?" Judy was referring to our Director of Student Health, Mary Mumford, a seasoned nurse.

"I'll call her," I responded as a scream billowed from the conference room, "AHHHHHHHH!" Judy grabbed the first aid kit and headed toward the pandemonium. "What's the first aid kit for?" I asked.

"No clue," Judy yelled back as she scurried out the door. I sat at her desk, baby in my arms, and looked up the number for Student Health. "Hello, Asbury Student Health Center, may I help you?" came the familiar voice of Mary Mumford.

"Mary, this is Doug. We need your help. We have a student... well no, I don't think she's a student, but a woman who is in labor over here in the Student Center. Judy is there, but we could really use your expertise!" Like the quintessential medical professional,

Mary didn't even pause to ask questions, "I'm on my way, Doug." And, *click*, she hung up.

"So Nurse Mumford's coming over?" Quacky asked, nervously.

"She is, Tina. But I wonder, maybe she would arrive sooner if she were picked up. Could you meet her in your cart and bring her here?"

"On my way, Doug!" Quacky huffed, buttoning her coat and straightening her hat. "I'll go get her right away!" As Quacky ran out the door, she nearly bowled over Jerry Ricardo, Asbury's Assistant Dean of Students and Director of Residence Life. I hadn't seen him all day. Jerry's a tall man, well over six feet, and in his down coat, wool hat, and ear muffs, his size was magnified. He pulled his scarf from his face and said, "Boss, it's a disaster out there!"

"It's pretty much a disaster in here, too," I quipped under my breath. "So, what's the latest?"

"Well, it looks like only about three-quarters of the students were actually able to go home from the residence halls. The others are stuck here."

"So we've got about 300 students stranded on-campus?" I asked, still rocking the baby in my arms.

"Yup, about that. And with all the roads closed, they're not leaving anytime soon. Holy shit, Doug-- what is that you're holding?"

"You're very observant," I jibed. "If he was a cobra, he would have killed you. He's a baby, and watch your language, please."

"Where did he come from?"

"Do I have to have the same conversation with you that Judy had with me?"

"Doug, I'm serious. Where did that baby come from, and what are you going to do with it?"

"Well, since you asked, he came from the manger and now we have to keep him in swaddling clothes."

"Doug!" Jerry said unzipping his coat, voice growing, "where did you get that baby?"

"Oh, you're no fun. Here's the scoop," I filled Jerry in. As I spoke, he finished taking off his outer gear and plunked down into one of the easy chairs. "Doug, can you get me something to drink?" he asked, "I'm pooped."

"Sure," I said, "let me get up, hoping not to disturb this sleeping baby and get you a beverage."

"I'm sorry," he said, leaning back and closing his eyes. "I'm just the most comfortable, and dry, that I've been all morning. I could probably take a nap right here." But then, Jerry's ever-so-brief respite was shattered by, "AWWWWWWW! GET IT OUT!" Jerry jumped up from his relaxed repose, "What the hell is that? There's a crazy person in the conference room!"

"Nah," I smirked. "She's not crazy, that I know of anyway, she's just in labor. Get ready for baby number two."

~7~

"**W**ho's having a baby? Who had *this* baby?

Doug, I'm not in the office for a morning and it's turned
into a maternity ward!" Jerry stood, exasperated. I was
having fun with Jerry, but a brief glimpse out the window
dampened my joviality. The snow was so heavy, the
window appeared to be shrouded by a billowing white
bed sheet. "Jerry, I will fill you in, not that I have all of
the answers, but I think we have to focus on getting the
Student Center ready for visitors."

"You mean our students from the halls?"

"Maybe, but if the power goes out, the town may
need the Student Center, and any other campus facility
we can muster to house residents from Ocean Grove.
Especially our senior citizens."

Jerry nodded, "I'll check to see what bedding we have on-hand. We're storing all of the blankets and pillows that conference services uses during their summer programs next door in the multi-purpose room. We don't have cots, but as I said, we do have blankets and pillows. Do you really think people will need to sleep here?"

"We should prepare for it… sleeping and eating. Can you check with Gene in food service to see how we might handle feeding our 250 students plus members of the community?"

"Doug, Gene will stroke."

"I know that he's excitable, but we've got to be prepared. It doesn't need to be gourmet. Some soup, peanut butter and jelly, coffee, tea. Again, we've got to be prepared in case the power goes out." And as quickly as I uttered those words, it did.

****

As soon as the lights in the office went dark, they sputtered back to life. "I think we better be prepared, Jerry. At minimum, we've got to keep our students fed and warm. If the power stays on, they can eat in either the Student Center Cafeteria or the Dining Hall, whichever Gene prefers, they can sleep in their rooms. If the power goes out, we may need to relocate everyone to the Campus Center, it will be warmer and we'll have the emergency generators running for a while, at least. If we have to host folks from the village of Ocean Grove, that will change everything."

"Don't our students get priority, Doug? They pay tuition," Jerry sounded uncharacteristically cynical.

"In an emergency, Jerry, we can't think about that. If someone gets mad because we fed a family hotdogs paid by tuition dollars, let them complain. We'll figure it out. We've got to do the right thing."

Jerry looked embarrassed, "I didn't mean that we wouldn't take care of people, Doug, I just…"

"I know you didn't," I said, adjusting the baby in my arms who seemed on the verge of waking up. "Just see what our possibilities are. While you do that, I'll look after this little guy, and Judy will look after our impending mom in the other room."

"Judy's delivering the baby?"

"If Quacky doesn't bring Mary here soon, she just might."

"Let me go talk to Gene. I don't know nothin' about birthin' babies."

"Thanks. And if I see Scarlet or Rhett, I'll let them know about your limitations." As Jerry walked out of the suite, a snow-covered, parka-laden person entered. Waving rapidly, the person's mittened hands flapped with excitement. Jerry and I both looked at the spectacle, speechless. The waving continued. As Jerry backed away, I said, "can we help you?"

Immediately the arms started pulling at the muffler wrapped around its neck. For a second I worried that it was being smothered by the wool. "Isssss mmeeeeeeeee!" came a voice hidden deep within the depth of much fabric. "Isssssss mmmmmeeeeeeee!" I looked at Jerry, and he shook his head. He didn't have any idea who this was or what they were saying, either.

"Do we know you?" I asked, still juggling the baby. The figure continued to remove its muffler and yank away its hood from the face, "It's me!" she called. "Ronnie!"

"Ronnie?" Jerry responded to his steadfast administrative assistant, "What are you doing here?"

"Well it's a work day, isn't it, and I've been working all day to get here!"

"I didn't expect you," Jerry stated. "Aren't the roads closed? You live in Holmdel!"

"They're closed now, but they weren't when I left at 7:00. By the time I got to Red Bank, traffic was already backed up. By the time I got to Tinton Falls, the roads were starting to get slick. And by the time I got to Cedar Avenue in W. Long Branch, the roads were impassable. I parked in the McDonald's down the street and walked here!"

"Since you were there, you could have at least brought some fries," Jerry smirked.

"I've got your fries," Ronnie sneered. Ronnie might have looked like a fifties housewife, replete with ruffled collar and pearls, but she had the wit of a sailor. "And I'll stuff them up your... Doug? What are you holding?"

"It's a baby," I responded.

"I see that it's a baby. Where did you get it?"

"In the manger," I responded matter-of-factly. The joke never got old.

"And I suppose He was wrapped in swaddling clothes?"

"So you've heard of him?"

"And were there angels near saying, 'Glory to God in the highest, and on earth peace, good will toward men?' Doug, I'm Irish Catholic, I know the story. Where did you get that baby?"

"That's really the $64,000 question. It seems that *this* one belongs to a young woman from either Asbury or

Long Branch, or close by. We've not located his mother yet."

"*This one*? Are there *more*?" Ronnie asked.

"Maybe," Jerry replied. "Just go into the conference room…" Ronnie threw her winter garments down and rushed to the conference room. As Jerry and I chit-chatted, Ronnie rushed back a few moments later, "Doug, do you see what's going on in there?"

"Not if I can help it," I offered.

"No! Not in the conference room, but over there!" Ronnie pointed to the large multi-purpose room outside of our office. I looked, and witnessed a steady stream of people, mostly senior citizens, entering the empty space. I stood quickly, gawking at our new guests. "Jerry, we better get those blankets quick. And we've got to get to Gene. We have holiday guests!"

~8~

Before I moved, I heard my name being called

and knew that I was in trouble. "Doug! Doug! I need you!" It was Miss Bettie, the Campus Center's beloved, and territorial, custodian. Miss Bettie had come to New Jersey from Arkansas in the early seventies and never left. She raised her family on her salary from cleaning facilities at Asbury College. She was respected, revered, and in certain times, feared.

"I'm in here, Miss Bettie!" I called. Like everyone else, she was bundled like an Eskimo. She came into the office suite, put her hand on her hip and asked, "What is going on, here?"

"I'm not sure how to answer that question, Bettie," I responded, still jiggling.

"And *what* do you have in your arms?" she said, placing her other hand on her other hip.

"Everyone seems to be asking that, too," I replied. "It's a baby."

"I know it's a baby. Why do you have it? And why are all these people coming in and messing up my Student Center?"

"The answer to your first question is, 'because he needs someone to hold him.' The answer to your second question is, I'm not sure-- but Jerry, here, is ready to help you figure that out. By the way, where have you been?"

"Doug! You know that on move out day we are all over in the residence halls cleaning! But since so many kids are still here because of the storm, I came back here. I thought it'd be quiet, but boy was I wrong!"

"And you haven't even gone into the conference room," Jerry offered.

"What's wrong with the conference room?" Bettie said, a bit more agitated, "did someone mess up my conference room? I just cleaned it yesterday!"

"Well, we've had some developments today," I shared, looking toward the conference room.

"Well if someone messed it up, it's going to stay messed up," Bettie said, moving toward the room.

"I wouldn't go in there if I were you," Jerry yelled. But it was too late. Within seconds Bettie ran back to us, "*Doug*! Do you know what's happening in there?"

"I'm trying to ignore it," I said.

"You can't ignore it! There's going to be a baby in there… and by the looks of things, Judy's already full of a mess. What are we going to do?"

"Judy is going to handle the baby in the conference room until Mary arrives," I tried to soothe, "Ronnie's going to take care of this little guy, and Jerry and I are going to see what we can do to make all of the community members and students comfortable." I turned and handed the baby to Ronnie, "But first, I need to go to the bathroom."

****

As I walked out of the suite to make my pit stop, I heard a familiar voice, "Dean Doug, can I help?" I turned, and saw a woman in a red cloak.

"Hi," I said. "Didn't I meet you in the Post Office this morning?"

"You are such a charmer," she said, pulling the cloak from her face to reveal her white curls. "My apartment in town lost its water. So they suggested that I come here. I hate to be useless."

"I realize that I never caught your name?"

"Jessica. Jessica Clouse."

"Well, very nice to meet you Mrs. Clouse. And depending on how long everyone will be stuck here, we'll need everyone's help sooner or later. In fact, I'm about to go downstairs and speak with our director of dining services. People are going to get hungry pretty quickly. But if you'll excuse me just a moment," I said, heading toward the men's room.

"You had better hurry, they're going to need you in there, soon," Jessica said pointing to the conference room.

"I'm sorry?" I responded quizzically. Was she timing my bathroom break?

"They're going to need your help, that's all." I continued to look curiously, as the lights flickered again and then finally went fully dark, plummeting the Campus Center into obscurity. As a few meager emergency lights sputtered to life, emitting about 30 watts of light, I heard Judy's frantic cry. "Doug! Doug! I need you, please, hurry!"

I looked at the stranger who smiled wisely, "See? I told you."

****

I forgot that nature was calling and ran toward the conference room to find Jessica standing in the doorway. "Dean Doug! Judy needs help!" I ran in and found Judy sitting in a chair eye-level to Stephanie's spread legs as she lay on the conference room table.

"Judy, is everything alright?"

"Doug, this baby is coming and I can't see. I need the flashlight from the back room and I need you to hold it for me!"

"But Mary's on her way," I sputtered and Judy interrupted. "We can wait for Mary, and if she comes, she's going to need the light too."

"Ahhhhhhhhhhh! It hurts! It hurts!" came Stephanie's shrieks.

"Doug, hurry!"

I ran back to the office suite into the copy room and grabbed an industrial-size flashlight that we kept for emergencies. I clicked the button and luckily, a strong beam of light followed. "Is everything okay, Doug?" Ronnie asked holding baby number 1. "I don't know," I said heading out the door, "Judy says that the baby is coming fast and she needs a light," I paused and looked at Ronnie holding the baby. "Why can't one of the kids hold the flashlight? Or, I'll trade ya," I swallowed.

"Not on your life. Go in there, Doctor."

"I'm not that kind of doctor."

"Get in there, Judy needs you. YOU, Doug. I'm sure Judy will feel better with another adult, especially you, in the room with her."

I turned and went to the conference room. I was nervous, scared even, but knew that Ronnie was right. I needed to be there for Judy (at least until Mary arrived.) I clicked on the light and the beam illuminated the dim room. Even though it was the middle of the day, and the conference room blinds were open, the storm was shrouding the windows with dense blasts of snow.

"Ovuh he-ya," Judy called to me. "I need you to point the light toward her vagina." There was something that I wouldn't have expected to hear as I started my day, or ever! "Uh, okay," I obliged, trying not to look directly at Stephanie's privates.

"Much bettah," Judy announced. "Stephanie, if you need to push, you need to push. Kids, hold her hands and help her!"

"I need to push!" Stephanie screamed as Jessica and Charley grabbed one of her hands.

"Then PUSH!" Judy instructed, looking like an umpire at home plate. "PUSH, Stephanie, you can do this!"

"This SUCKSSSSSSSSSSSSSS!," Stephanie screamed, as Jessica held her left hand tighter. "I don't think I can do this, make it stop. I'm going to stop!"

"You can't stop, Stephanie-- your baby needs you. Keep going. When the next contraction happens, PUSH! You're almost finished!" As Judy coached, and I held the light, I could see a bulbous object pulsing from Stephanie's intimate sanctum. I knew that it was the baby's head ready to emerge.

"C'mon, Stephanie," I called, surprising myself. "Your baby is ready to join the world… let's make it happen!" Immediately after saying it, I felt like a cheap football announcer.

"AHHHHHHHHHHH!" Stephanie screamed. "I can't do this!"

"You are doing it, Stephanie... c'mon... one more push," Judy coached. "Let's go. One, Two, Three, PUSH!"

"AHHHHHHHHHHH," Stephanie screamed again, and through the beam of light I was shining on her privates, I saw a baby's head fully emerge. "Push again," Judy called, hands ready to catch the precious cargo. "Push again, Stephanie, you are almost they-uh!" Judy's Brooklyn accent was even more pronounced under stress.

"UGHHHHHHHHH," Stephanie screamed, and as she did, I saw Judy hunker down and embrace the baby that came from Stephanie's body. Judy scooped the baby into a blanket, and after a few seconds, the room was filled with the cries of an infant.

"You did it, Stephanie," Judy called, swaddling the baby in an SG tee-shirt. "You did it. You have a beautiful baby girl!" The students in the room, originally looking pale and terrified, cheered. As did I. Judy had saved the day, and Stephanie's baby.

"You were amazing, Judy," I responded. "Just amazing." Judy stood, her navy blue dress greased with bio-products. Judy moved toward Stephanie and handed her her baby, "Here she is… and she's gorgeous!" Stephanie gathered her baby and looked at her quizzically, "she's mine? Really?"

"All yours, Stephanie, and she's beautiful," Judy smiled. "Congratulations." As everyone in the room seemed to breathe a sigh of relief, I worried about cutting the umbilical cord, feeding the baby, and other life-saving, if not warm and fuzzy, implementations.

"We're here!" came a huffy voice. Quacky, splattered with snow, rammed into the room as Mary Mumford trailed behind, "Let's birth this baby!"

"You're a little late, Tina," I said. "The baby has been birthed. Take a look." I pointed toward Stephanie, who was cradling her baby with Jessica and Charley looking on. I didn't have to say anything to Mary, who rushed into the room and began assessing the situation. As she took over supervision, I sidled toward Judy, "You were amazing."

"When you've had as many kids as I have, this was easy."

"Don't sell yourself short," I said. "Having babies is one thing. Delivering them is another. You made a miracle happen today, Judy. You should be proud." Judy looked at me, still covered in pre and post baby slop, and for the first time ever, melted. She sank into my arms and said, "I was so scay-uhed." She rested her head on my shoulder, "What if there had been a complication? I don't know what I would've done, Doug!" I hugged her, relishing in all of the reasons why I valued Judy Wessler so highly. "You were brilliant, Judy," I said, still hugging her. "It doesn't matter what *could* have happened, you made the birth of Stephanie's baby become a reality. You made a miracle happen." Judy looked up at me, primped her jet-black bouffant and said, "I *was* pretty good, *wasn't* I?"

"You were better than good," I chuckled, "you were incredible."

"We think so, too!" Came an elderly voice from behind us. Judy and I turned simultaneously and saw a crowd of twenty or so senior citizens smiling and then clapping. "We heard the commotion and couldn't believe that someone was actually in labor!" said a man with white hair and big mustache. "You created a miracle, madam!" Judy blushed, which was a rare occurrence, and rested her head on my shoulder. "See," I said, "I told you so."

As Judy walked over to her newly found fans, Charley approached me, "Dean Doug?"

"Hi, Charley, is something wrong?"

"I don't know, it's just that... the baby."

"She's beautiful, isn't she?"

"No, I mean yes, but not *that* baby." Poor Charley looked tortured, "if Stephanie just had her baby, who had the baby that we found in the manger?"

I wondered that myself, but tried to be reassuring, "Right now, all we can do is be thankful that they're safe. We'll figure it out, Charley." And in my head, I hoped that I was right.

~9~

With the baby born and Mary Mumford and

Quacky in control, I realized that I still needed to find out if Jerry touched base with Gene to see how we were going to feed people. I grabbed my phone and dialed Jerry.

"We've got some trouble, boss," came Jerry's shaky voice.

"Story of my day," I responded, woefully. "What's the problem?"

"Gene's staff left."

"What do you mean, left?"

"Left! They're gone! When they heard that we were in a state of emergency, they left. I'm with Gene in the Dining hall… and it's only the two of us! Plus, we don't have power or generators over here."

"But we do have generators over here, at least for now," I replied. "We're going to have to feed people here in the Student Center. Ask Gene if we have enough food over here to feed about 350 people."

"350?"

"You said that we've got about 250 students who couldn't go home and we've got about 100 senior citizens from the community. Not to mention us!" I heard Jerry's muffled voice as he relayed the message to Gene, who was excitable on a normal day. I heard something like a yell, and then Jerry came back, "Gene and I are coming over to the Student Center to assess… Gene thinks we'll be okay for tonight."

"Okay, I'll meet you down there."

"But, Doug, remember, Gene's staff is gone. We're going to have to do the cooking."

"I'll wear my apron. We can do this."

"See you in a few, or twenty. I've never seen snow like this. There's eight more inches on the ground and the guys plowed a half hour ago."

"Be safe," I said, hanging up. As I did, I headed downstairs to the Student Center cafeteria. I walked down the cement stairs to the glorious smell of food. As roasted turkey, bacon, pizza and other delicious scents wafted my way, I wondered who was cooking if Gene's staff had left campus? I peered beyond the deserted cash registers toward the kitchen and saw Miss Bettie and Jessica Clouse busily stirring and basting.

"What are you doing?" I asked, mouth ajar.

"Cooking. Someone's got to," Miss Bettie replied, not turning away from the pot she was stirring. "It was actually Jessica's idea." Jessica turned from checking one of the ovens and wiped her hands on the Asbury College apron wrapped around her middle. "I told you that I didn't like to be useless, so I saw Bettie, and we discussed the need to get some food ready, and here we are!"

"But I was thinking sandwiches. Peanut butter and jelly, it looks like the two of you are going gourmet!"

"I don't do peanut butter and jelly," Miss Bettie said still stirring. "Since we have real food, we're going to cook it. See? The kids are already coming in." I turned, and saw about fifteen snow-soaked students enter the Student Center. I looked at my watch, and it was approaching 4pm. Almost dinner time.

"Hi, everyone," I said. "How are you all doing?"

"Okay, I guess," one beleaguered young woman responded. "We're cold, and we wanted to go home for Christmas, but I guess we can't complain."

"Yeah," chimed in another student. "I was supposed to be on a plane to meet my family in St. Croix. That's not happening anytime soon. The only beach I'm going to see is the one down the street, and that's covered in two feet of snow."

"Well come on in," I said, ushering them inside the cafeteria. "It's not St. Croix, or home, but you're with friends and these women have prepared some great food. Why don't you grab some coffee or hot chocolate and dry off. We'll let you know when dinner's ready." The students complied, unzipping parkas and abandoning gloves to grab hot drinks. "Where do we pay?" asked a student in an Asbury College knit hat.

"It's all on me," I said. "Merry Christmas."

"I'm Jewish," one bundled student responded. "Still on me," I said. "Happy fill your belly with warmth, then. Chanukah's over, so we'll have to improvise." The students didn't seem to care one way or another and grabbed their drinks and headed toward the tables in the cafeteria. As I looked into the space, I was charmed by the warm glow of votive candles in glass holders at every table. "Where did the candles come from?" I called toward Miss Bettie and Jessica.

"Oh, that was my idea," Jessica replied sheepishly. "I just thought it would add a nice touch."

"They do," I responded, "but where'd we get them?"

"No worries, Dean," Jessica answered. "I picked them up along the way." I was about to ask her where, when Jerry and Gene barreled into the Student Center. "We're in trouble, Doug," Gene called. "We may be out of food soon!"

****

"What do you mean out of food?" I asked incredulously. "Bettie and Jessica have been cooking up a storm—I mean, no pun intended."

Gene, shoulders laden with an inch of snow gaped at me, "What are they cooking? This kitchen was just about empty as of last night, I made sure of it in advance of the break."

"I don't know, but they're cooking. Doesn't it smell great? Maybe the senior citizens brought groceries with them?"

"Enough for 300 people?!" Gene seemed disturbed. I walked over to the grill where Miss Bettie and Jessica were cooking and asked, "Where did all of this food come from?"

Miss Bettie looked at me, "Gene's crazy. The walk-in cooler is stocked. There's meat, vegetables, cheese, bread dough, anything we could want."

"But where did it come from," Gene called over my shoulder, more disturbed than relieved.

"I don't know, Gene," Miss Bettie replied putting her hand on her hip, "it was in *your* cooler!" As a potential fracas was about to ensue, I looked at Jessica who was quietly humming and stirring and not making eye contact. I walked around the fighting Miss Bettie and Gene and closed in on Jessica, "Do you know where all of the food came from?" I asked. She sniffed, and did not make eye contact, "Oh, Dean Doug, of course not. I mean, I brought a few things from my apartment, but sometimes the most important questions aren't the most obvious."

"I'm sorry?" I asked.

"Sometimes, although the most obvious questions are the lowest hanging fruit to answer, they are not the most important. I bet that there are other questions that are more important than how we were blessed with this food."

I just stared at her, hoping she would share the question that was more important. She pushed a white curl from her face and then she did, "you know the mom of the second baby, Dean Doug, but who is the mom who abandoned the first?"

~10~

As the students began filing in for dinner en masse and the senior citizens joined from upstairs, the cafeteria gained a warm and energetic vibe. Everyone was eating off of paper plates, not sustainable, but all we had, and a festive spirit emanated through the space. From table to table, different Christmas carols could be heard being played on individual iPhones and the random and reckless joy added to the jovial ambiance. I had never heard a remix of "O Come all Ye Faithful," "Rudolph the Rednosed Reindeer," and NSYNC's, "Happy Holidays," sound so beautiful.

I saw Judy sitting in a booth with Ronnie, Jimmy, and Mary cooing at the babies and enjoying their meal. Quacky and Gene were surveying the crowd, each popping fresh-baked cookies into their mouths. Despite the blizzard, that was still raging, and the 300 people stranded at Asbury College, life was good. The only thing that would have made it better for me was to have my wife, Barbara, and son, Ethan, with me, but I was glad that they were safe and warm a few blocks away at home.

I walked around the room, relishing in the unexpected holiday cheer. Students chatting with senior citizens from the community, the scene looked like something Norman Rockwell might have painted. As I continued to walk around the room, I did notice one young man, sitting by himself in a booth looking at Judy's table and the babies. His light African-American skin contrasted against his dark grey puffy coat, and I thought I saw him wipe a tear from his eye. As he sat among the more prominent din, I thought of Jessica's words, "Sometimes, although the most obvious questions are the lowest hanging fruit to answer, they are not the most important." In all of the frivolity and excitement of the day, I could have easily missed him.

I approached him still not recognizing his face. "Hi," I said as I got closer. "How are you doing?" He stood immediately, "I was just getting something to eat," he said. "I'll be on my way."

"Hey," I said surprised, "you don't have to leave, I just don't recognize you. Are you a student at AC?"

"I don't need this," he responded nervously. "I just wanted to make sure, I wasn't sure..." he continued to be distracted by something at Judy's table. Then, I knew.

"That's your son," I said.

"Why would you say that?" he came back defensively.

"Because I know that look. He's your boy. But how..." I stopped myself, because I remembered that sometimes, although the most obvious questions are the lowest hanging fruit to answer, they are not the most important. "Go to him," I said. "I'll take you."

"Daddy!" came a call from across the dining room. I turned and saw Barbara and Ethan, bundled to the hilt, dripping with snow and looking to me like angels. "Ethan!" I yelled and he ran to me. I hugged and kissed his six year old chilly face and said, "Did you and mommy walk here?"

"Yeah! It was real fun. She didn't want to, but I wanted to make sure that you were alright. Have you seen all of the snow? It's taller than me!"

" I'm sure it is!" I said. "Do you want something to eat? Some hot chocolate?" Barbara joined us and gave me a kiss, "he would not relent. He had to make sure you were okay."

"I'm glad he did," I said, hugging her again. I was distracted by the new dad standing in front of me, still staring at his baby. "Why don't you go get Ethan some cocoa and a cookie," I said. Barbara looked at me knowingly, "*is* everything alright?"

"I think it will be," I said, giving her another kiss. She grabbed Ethan who voluntarily joined her for treats and I stepped up closer to my new dad. "You never stop being their dad," I said. "And the joy, and the hefty responsibility never goes away, either. But did you see my son's face? I would do anything for that boy. He is mine. He is part of me. I wouldn't give that up for anything." My friend looked toward the ground, and then wiped another tear.

"What's your name?" I asked.

"Marcus," he replied. And without asking him anymore questions, he volunteered, "We live in Asbury Park. Morgan, she's my girlfriend, had the baby and then freaked out. She left. She bolted. I didn't know what to do… and the hospital was too far to walk, so I brought him here."

"But why did you leave him in the chapel?" I asked.

"I wasn't thinking right, and I had to leave him someplace where he would be found. Since it was Christmas, I thought that the chapel was the best place- all eyes are on the manger this time of year." Marcus was right, but he didn't take into consideration that we were closing for Christmas break. He was lucky that there were students who were actually still around to find, and save, his son.

"Do you want to hold him," I asked, touching his back. He bristled just a little, "can I?"

"He's your son," I said, "let me introduce you." We walked slowly toward Judy and Ronnie's table like a bride walking down the aisle. I suppose the commitment was no less great, probably more so. We both stood at the head of the table, and I said, "Hi, everyone. This is Marcus."

"Hello, Marcus," Judy and Ronnie said in unison. Then they both looked at me expectantly.

"Ronnie," I said, "Marcus is this baby's father... and he'd like to hold him." Ronnie looked at me, then at Judy, and began to stand. As she stood, she eyed-up Marcus, and again, looked at Judy and then me, "This is a very special baby," she said, "who deserves the best." I smiled at Ronnie who seemed to take that as approval, and she handed the baby to Marcus.

"The baby also deserves to be called a girl," Judy chimed-in still jiggling the other bundle of joy. "He's a she." Marcus looked at all of us and then broke out in laughter, "Morgan's friend bundled him... her up, and I

never saw for sure. I just assumed he was a, well, a he."
Marcus held his daughter, appropriately scrutinized by
Judy and Ronnie, and Ethan ran over to me.

"Daddy, where did *those* come from?"

"What, Ethan?"

"Those presents?" Ethan said, pointing to an
abundance of packages that I had not seen sitting under
the Christmas tree in the cafeteria.

"I don't know, Ethan, I don't remember seeing
them before?"

"Mrs. Jessica told me that they were there," Ethan
offered. "Before she left, she said that there were
presents. Some for us kids, some for needy people in
Ocean Grove. She said that they were all labeled." I
looked around, not sure what I was looking for. "Mrs.
Jessica," I asked, "you said she left?"

"Yup," he said matter-of-factly, "she gave me a
cookie and said that she had to leave. She said that there
was lots to do."

"Did she say where she was going?" I asked.

"Nope, just that I should show you the presents and thank you."

"Thank me?"

"Yup," Ethan said, snuggling closer. "Thank you for, uh, she said it, thank you for, looking for the most oblivious questions."

"Oblivious?" I asked, perplexed.

"Yup, that's what I think she said," Ethan wondered. "O-B-V-I-O-U-S. Oblivious questions."

I took him in my arms and hugged him as tightly as I could. Obvious. While some things were not obvious, as I had learned during the past twenty-four hours, other things were. Like a community banding together during a tough time, the staff and students of Asbury College pulling through, and my family. I knew that my love for my family during this holiday blizzard in Ocean Grove was one of the most OBVIOUS things of all.

-THE END-

Author, Heath P. Boice

A college administrator for twenty years, Heath P. Boice knows about college life. He takes this experience and uses it as the foundation form his unique series of "cozy" novels. This is the first Ocean Grove "Short" Mystery that pays homage to Boice's former home, Ocean Grove, New Jersey.

Heath has received both regional and national recognition for his professional work in college administration, boasting over 50 publications and convention presentations on topics including: Legal Issues, Student

Affairs around the Globe, and Service Leadership and Innovation in higher education.

Heath holds a Bachelor of Arts in Public Communications (radio/television) and a Master of Science in Education in College Student Personnel and Counseling from the College of Saint Rose in Albany, New York. He also holds a Doctorate in Education from Rutgers University, New Brunswick, New Jersey. A lifelong learner, Heath also earned an Advanced Graduate Certificate in Service Leadership and Innovation from Rochester Institute of Technology (RIT) in Rochester, New York.

Heath has had a successful career as a college dean, administrator, and instructor at both private and public universities, most recently as the Associate Vice President for Student Affairs and Community Development at RIT. He also teaches graduate courses linking higher education and customer service in RIT's College of Applied Science and Technology, a unique program that he developed. Additionally, Heath serves as a faculty member in the School of Advanced Studies, University of Phoenix.

Before working in higher education, Heath worked both on and off air at radio and television stations as a news anchor, writer, producer, and feature talk show host. When not working with college students or writing, Heath enjoys spending time with his wife and daughters in their Rochester, New York home. He also enjoys gardening, cooking, and reading… mostly mysteries.

For more about Heath P. Boice, visit www.101mysteries.com

A note from the author:

Hello, dear reader. I hope that you enjoyed this adventure in Ocean Grove. I assume that you found this mystery because you love the town of Ocean Grove, the Jersey Shore, or both. Thank you for choosing this book. I love to hear feedback! Please be sure to send me a note at Heath@101mysteries.com or write a review on Amazon.com. Your thoughts will help guide future Ocean Grove Mysteries.

Best,

Heath